PENGUIN BOOKS
LANTERNS ACROSS THE SNOW

Susan Hill was born in Scarborough, Yorkshire, in 1942. She was educated at grammar schools there and in Coventry, and studied at King's College, London. Her works include *Gentleman and Ladies*, *A Change for the Better*, *I'm the King of the Castle* (Somerset Maugham Prize), *The Albatross and Other Stories* (John Llewelyn Rhys Memorial Prize), *Strange Meeting*, *The Bird of Night* (Whitbread Award), *A Bit of Singing and Dancing*, *In the Springtime of the Year* and *The Woman in Black*, as well as the illustrated *Shakespeare Country* and *The Spirit of the Cotswolds*. She has also written books for children, *One Night at a Time*, *Mother's Magic* and *Can It Be True?* (Smarties Prize), and two autobiographical books, *The Magic Apple Tree* and *Family*. In addition she has edited Thomas Hardy's *The Distracted Preacher and Other Tales* for the Penguin Classics and is a regular broadcaster and book reviewer for various journals and newspapers.

Susan Hill is married to the Shakespeare scholar Stanley Wells, and they have two daughters and live in the Oxfordshire countryside.

From Jenny

Xmas '91.

LANTERNS ACROSS THE SNOW

SUSAN HILL

with wood engravings by
Kathleen Lindsley

PENGUIN BOOKS

PENGUIN BOOKS

Published by the Penguin Group
27 Wrights Lane, London W8 5TZ, England
Viking Penguin Inc., 40 West 23rd Street, New York, New York 10010, USA
Penguin Books Australia Ltd, Ringwood, Victoria, Australia
Penguin Books Canada Ltd, 2801 John Street, Markham, Ontario, Canada L3R 1B4
Penguin Books (NZ) Ltd, 182–190 Wairau Road, Auckland 10, New Zealand

Penguin Books Ltd, Registered Offices: Harmondsworth, Middlesex, England

First published by Michael Joseph, 1987
Published in Penguin Books 1989
1 3 5 7 9 10 8 6 4 2

Reproduced, printed and bound in Great Britain by
BPCC Hazell Books Ltd
Member of BPCC Ltd
Aylesbury, Bucks, England
Filmset in Ehrhardt

For Jenny

CONTENTS

PREFACE

LAST NIGHT, the snow fell. And then I began to remember. I remembered all the things that I had forgotten. Or so it had seemed.

But not forgotten after all. They were all there, stored away like treasures.

Last night, the snow fell.

The sky had been darkening all afternoon, growing greyer and greyer, and swelling with snow. It must have been cold, too, bitter cold. You could see that it was cold. In here, I am never cold; there is always a small fire, even in summer. It's a small room, and rather dark, but brightened by the fire. The fire is quite enough.

I sit by the window until it is dark – every day. And so I *saw* the cold, the air freezing.

There is a tree outside, one tree. Its branches are bare now. They bow down just beside my window, and the birds come – a sparrow, a robin, a blue tit, quick, quick, quick. And there is one bush, set against the wall, all scattered about with winter flowers, like bright, bright stars.

Beyond this window, where I sit, there is a little backyard. With my tree, the flowering bush, the little birds. And I can look up between the houses, and see the sky.

Last night, the snow fell, and then I began to remember. There is no one else left now, no one who remembers it all. Mother and Father are long dead. And brother Will, gone for a soldier, brother Will dead, too.

And Nancy in the Rectory kitchen; and Sam Hay, who whistled through the gap in his teeth and put up the swing for me on the apple tree bough in the garden. And m'lord at the Hall, and his lady, and their pale-faced, pale-haired daughter whose frock I so envied, and whose eyes were the colour of sea-washed stones, and who said to me, that Christmas time, quietly in a corner, 'I am a disappointment to them, because I am not a son.'

I told my mother, who frowned. 'But *you* are precious,' she said.

And old Betsy Barlow with one leg. Pether the Churchwarden, and Mr Vale the verger, Father's right hand.

And his curate, with the bobbing Adam's-apple, and a new, new wife who smiled at me, and took my hand beside the Christmas tree, and smiled again – at Father, at Mother, at the curate, at brother Will, but spoke not a single word. And died, the next year, with her daughter Rachel, in childbirth. And the curate went away.

They are all dead, now.

And those from the village who came to church. And those who did not – but Father cared for them all.

I remember the great, bleak, brown-turfed Dorset barrows, with the buzzards soaring and circling above. The tiny cottages dark with smoke and crowded with children. The servants at the Hall, crammed into cold attic rooms, never having a space for themselves, or hot water to wash in. The old men and women with thin hair and thin legs, and bent backs and no teeth, sitting on steps in the sun, or snug on settle-seats beside the fire, content among the washing and the bubbling stoves, and their children's children's children. Or alone, in our village, or the next village beyond, or tucked away at the end of forgotten lanes, and never a soul went by. But Father would go, and take us with him. 'They should see for themselves,' he said.

There is no one else left who remembers.

But last night the snow fell. And I remembered. I will write it all down, now, before it's too late, too dark. For I am the last to remember.

I remember the days at the turn of the year, with the first buds pricking on the blackthorn hedge, and bending down to find a celandine between the blades of grass; remember the scudding sky and the hares running and racing across the hills, and Will after

13

them, far ahead of me, and Tip the terrier bounding beside; remember the swing, up, up, up, until I felt I would touch the floor of heaven.

Remember the hay-makers' bent brown backs, and the great tired horses hauling the wagons home with their golden load, and the men's voices calling to one another, down the lanes in the last of the light. And we stood beside the gate to watch them pass.

Remember the tops of the elms in the churchyard, being tossed by the winds of October, November, and the night one tree was brought down and lay like a giant, dead and fallen to earth, all jagged and ripped from its roots; and all the next night, the wind still roared and howled, and moaned and prowled around the house, rattling the latches, crying at my window to get in, so that I ran in fear to Will.

'Ghosts, ghosts! Ghosts in the graveyard.'

But, 'Hush, hush. Don't dare to wake Mother and Father. No ghosts, no ghosts,' Will said.

'Yes! Oh, yes!'

In a grave in the churchyard, beyond the window, we had two brothers. Dead, long dead.

'The wind. Only the wind,' said Will.

For never did winds blow as strong as they blew there, rushing across Ladyman Barrow, bending back the trees. It seemed to be the gathering place for all the winds of the world.

I remember.

I remember that we felt rich, *were* rich, when so many were poor. That our beds were soft at night, when the Son of Man had no place to lay his head, Father said, and others only the hard ground on which to sleep. That we were loved, when others were not; that we were warm, when out in the dark night-fields, the sheep and the cows, and the fox and the hares were all cold, and birds had been found with their feet frozen to branches. The pond and the ditches, the stream that flowed through the wood, turned all to ice, and stayed frozen and still for weeks and weeks on end. Forever, that winter seemed.

And out in their hovel, beyond Ladyman Barrow, an old man called Roberts and his poor, blind wife, died of being hungry, and cold, and ill, and alone. And Father never knew, not until too late. And he wept – our father, so proud, and respected; our father, grey and stern and upright, wept and raged, and pounded his fist, and cried to heaven for vengeance. 'Remember this,' he said, 'oh, you remember.'

Last night, the snow fell. And I began to remember.

Remember joy and sorrow, nights and days, summer and winter and fresh, sweet spring; remember the tall old house, and the swing on the apple tree bough. The years roll back to reveal my childhood, set in a magic circle, bright, bright, before the dark.

I sit here beside the window that looks onto the little backyard, and the tree, with the birds on its branches, and the bush, starry with flowers.

November, December.
And above, between the houses, the sky.
Last night, the snow fell. And then, I began to remember. Spring days and summer days, autumn and winter. Father and Mother, and brother Will. The house and the church, and the grass and the graves between. The days of my childhood.

But I remember that Christmas best of all . . .

CHRISTMAS EVE

'CHRISTMAS EVE,' Fanny said. 'Christmas Eve.' As if saying it aloud would make her better able to believe it. 'Christmas Eve,' and she watched her own breath puff out like pale smoke on the cold air of her bedroom, and turn to a fine mist on the windowpane.

Christmas Eve was the best of it all, the waiting and laughing, the sense of excitement through the house, like one of Nancy's black pots kept simmering. She thought of the rest of the day, and the evening to come, and saw a gleam of brightness cast forward from the blazing gold of Christmas Day, lancing towards her like the light streaming under the crack beneath a half-open door.

Christmas Day, Fanny thought, is like the room beyond that door, a bright, bright room, an Aladdin's cave of treasure; the tree with its candles and the banked-up fire all glowing, and the pile of shining presents, and the Christmas table, heavy with good things, the smells and the laughter and the love and,

19

oh, the bright brightness. But for now, she was standing just outside, in the waiting room, and the light from the room that was Christmas Day just reached her, just touched, and she could feel her heart beat very fast.

She was nine years old. She could clearly remember last Christmas, yet it might have been a thousand years ago, it lay so far in the past, beyond the dark days of early winter, beyond the lingering days of autumn, beyond the summer, too; the heat and the flowers and the running about with petticoats all hitched up over bare brown legs, and the weeks beside the sea. In August, Father took over a parish near Lyme where the churchyard and the Rectory garden sloped down to the path that led to the cliffs and the beach and the wide, wide bay. Brother Will had scrambled and climbed, and picked away for hours at the loose shale of the cliffs, digging for fossils. And finding them, too, chunks of blue-grey slate which opened like little hinged boxes to reveal the ammonite hidden beneath, coiled and ribbed like a snake. On the shingle were thousands of pebbles, and in among these they found treasures, tiny insects and animals, pressed into the hard stone, dead for a thousand years, Will said, and frail as paper shavings, but quite complete.

And they ran and ran across the great arc of the bay and the soles of their feet left watery moons on the sand, and the sky had been so blue, so blue, but darker where it merged with the sea. They had woken each morning at dawn, to creep from the house and down the cliff path, and where their hands and legs brushed against the grass clumps, butterflies flew up in puffs and fluttered out into the air, white, primrose and marvellous blue. Like angels, Fanny had thought, or like the souls of good people. But she had not said, only run faster, slip-slither down the last few yards after Will, and then onto the open beach, with the sea far out and glittering in the early sun, and the sand and the shingle pale, and the sky without clouds. And no one on earth but themselves.

Oh glory, glory! Fanny had said. And lifted her arms and spread them wide, and danced; then run, towards the gold and silver of the sea. Oh glory, glory!

Last Christmas was beyond that, beyond the whole of the summer and all the days of spring and another winter. She remembered everything about it, now it was come so close again, was almost here . . . If she reached out her hand far enough, stretched and stretched with the tips of her fingers, she would reach it.

She stood at the window, looking out. Christmas Eve; and the snow fell like goose-down.

Her room was at the top of the tall house, seventy stairs to the landing, and the last flight was steep and narrow and wound around. Will's room was farther down the narrow passage, and on the way there was a window, but it was placed too high for Fanny to see out. She could only look at a patch of sky, not even at the tops of the trees, elms and Scots pines, that stood beside the church. But her own window looked down on the garden and graveyard beyond, and the path that led to the small side door set in the wall of the church itself.

It had been snowing all day. It lay, softly piled over the earth and outlined the curve of each grey gravestone and covered the flat tops of the chest tombs

21

like quilts. The ledge outside her window was fat with snow. The church roof, the church porch, the bushes and the yew trees that stood, like statues in skirts, were soft with snow, and the sky was grey as a wolf's coat, and still it went on snowing.

Behind the church lay Ladyman Barrow, that wild, wild, open place, of strange sounds and keening winds and rare bird cries, furze and heather and scrub. Narrow paths criss-crossed, this way and that. You could be lost and wander for hours, days, out on the Barrow, you could die of thirst and heat and confusion, lie down on the rough ground and gladly die there, and never be found till your bones were white, Will said. Fanny was afraid of the Barrow, though Father walked across it for miles, on his visits to people who lived beyond. He strode out there, summer and winter, and knew every inch as well as those who'd been born beside it. He was never afraid on the Barrow, he said, never lonely or lost-feeling. God was always close. But it was that thought which Fanny did not like, though would never dare to have said.

On clear days, she could see the humped back of Ladyman Barrow from this window. On summer evenings, its outline was purple, the shadows between were lavender blue. On spring mornings, when the clouds raced, it dissolved into a pale mist, insubstantial, innocent, a place you might be happy on. Some days, it was only flat-grey, and dull, like a shape cut out of sugar-paper and pasted down onto the board of the sky.

Today, the swirling snow dazzled her, and the light was poor so she could not see the Barrow at all; for a moment, indeed, could barely see the church, a dozen yards away.

In the other direction, facing the Rectory, lay the village, and to the west, the wood, acre upon acre of dense dark trees, a private and dreadful place that crept right down to the very edge of the Rectory orchard, so that sometimes in the night, Fanny woke to hear the squeal of small creatures, the cries of fear and the hunt and the kill, and the shriek-shoosh of an owl.

M'lord's keeper set traps in that wood – Catchpole, a man Fanny hated and feared, who carried the soft bodies of dead animals hanging down from his bare hands and dripping blood; and always a gun, broken beneath his arm. Catchpole came this way too often; he stopped by the kitchen door to talk to Nancy, or to leave his terrible gifts, a rabbit, a pair of pearly-grey wood pigeons, a bead-eyed pheasant.

'May the Lord make us thankful,' Father said when they came to the table, and Fanny mumbled, and would have kept silent, and could have wept. But ate, all the same.

Suddenly, it had stopped snowing, the white world lay quite peaceful and still. And from down below, deep in the house, rich smells, voices calling, footsteps, a door closed. Christmas Eve.

Looking again from her high window, Fanny saw her father, tall and stooped and black as a crow in his black cloak, begin to walk across the deep snow of the churchyard, and from the grey stone tower of the church, the bell rang, dong-dong, dong-dong, dong-dong. Mr Vale the verger, ringing for Evensong. She could see the top of Father's head and his black shoulders, and as he made his way slowly through the billowed snow, a last flake or two came softly down, to rest on him.

There were deep pits made by his boots as he went, a line of them across the white of the snow. She watched him go diagonally between the graves, and then, as he always did, stop for a moment to look and bow his head, beside the place where her two brothers lay, the babies born and then dead long before Fanny ever was.

Then suddenly she wanted to go and be with him in the church, which by now would be decked out with all the green branches for Christmas Day. Wanted to walk out in the snow, and so she flew down the stairs like a bird, her feet barely touching each step, and the lower down she got, the richer and sweeter the smells were that wafted to meet her, plum pudding and baking, and oranges squeezed and cinnamon spice, and as she tumbled the last flight into the hall, the front door was flung open and in came Will, with Sam Hay, in a great white flurry of snow and cold air, bearing the log for the Christmas fire, and each of them draped in sheaves and swathes of green, their shoulders hung all about with branches and swags, of fir and spruce and ivy. They dropped them in piles on the floor, stamping their feet and blowing on fingers, and leaving snow to melt into pools on the clean polished floor.

Then out again, Will ahead. 'Now for the mistletoe bough!'

'Oh Mother!' she shouted, 'Mother!' so that from the back of the house her mother came, rustle and busy-ness and seeming to be encircled with secrets in store.

'They've gone for the mistletoe bough!' and Fanny ran into the drawing-room, up to the long windows that let onto the front lawn and the drive beyond, and from there, she could just see Will, climbing, climbing fast up the oldest oak, while Sam Hay stood below and waited. 'The mistletoe bough!'

But her mother had gone, back again into the farthest room of the house and her secrets, and Fanny knew why, because Will was climbing the great oak and their mother knew she must never prevent him, but nor could she ever bear to watch. Only Will would not fall, Will was like a cat, Will could climb anything.

From near the top of the tree, a sudden swift movement down to the ground, as the mistletoe bough fell onto the snow, and then, in a moment, another, a soft heap of pale green and milky white, gleaming slightly in the light that shone out from the window.

Fanny went back from the drawing-room into the hall, and stared at the Yule-log and the mounds of glistening green, touched her finger to the hard red berries of holly, and the pad of her thumb to a tiny spine. Then the front door came suddenly open again and, startled, jumping back, she felt the prick in her flesh and, looking down, saw already the bead of bright blood.

From below stairs, the crash of a tin pan.

At the kitchen table, Nancy, fat and floury and strong, stirred brandy into a bowl of dark and glistening fruit.

'Fingers out, I thank you, Miss Fanny Hart.'

On the old chair beside the range, Nelson the orange cat stirred deep in his sleep and extended his paws and his claws, and settled softly back inside himself.

Fanny leaned on the table's edge, and half closed her eyes, sniffing up the sugary spicy fruity mincemeat smell, reached out a hand and began to roll a lemon that lay there, to and fro, to and fro, until, quite unexpectedly, it rolled away from her and fell plop onto the stone-flagged floor.

'Fingers *out*, Miss Fanny!'

Fanny ran.

'Child, child!' as she almost crashed into her mother, coming through the hall.

'May I go to Father? I want to go to the church by myself. I want to be out in the snow.'

'Child, child!' but her mother was laughing. 'Boots, then, and coat and bonnet and warmest scarf.'

Oh, oh, hurry. Buttons and strings and hooks, all anyhow. Oh hurry, hurry.

'Perhaps, after all, Will had better. . . .'

Fanny ran. Through the hall, and down the dark passage between the coats to the heavy back door. Pulled it open slowly. And stood there for a moment, to catch her breath and grow calm, before stepping out. And all the world was white. Click, the door behind her, and then, oh then, into the snow. It creaked as she moved through it, and blew up a little, dry as powder, and quite firm to the touch of her hand.

Oh, glory, glory!

She began to make her way across the churchyard with infinite care, wanting to disturb as little as possible of the perfect snow.

It was cold. It was absolutely still. Quiet, so quiet, she could hear the pant of her own breathing, in, out, and the silky shuffle and squeak of her boots, pushing forward. She stopped. The air smelled cold. Tasted cold in her mouth. Above her head, the sky was clearing, and she could see a few stars pricking out between the parting clouds. There would be moonlight, then, and no more snow tonight. A bone-white, frozen, beautiful world.

She touched her hand to a gravestone and snow toppled off and fell on snow, soft as roses. Underneath, the rough grey stone, the lettering all worn away and mouldy with moss; she liked the shape of the gravestones. And out here, among them, close to all those sleepers under the earth, she was not afraid. There were no ghosts.

Ahead, lights flickering out from the windows of the church. Behind, the golden glow from the windows of the house.

Christmas Eve, Fanny thought, and drew in her breath for joy.

Then she went on. But instead of making her own track any further through the untouched snow, now she began to fit her feet into the deeper hollows made earlier by her father, and it was much easier, and somehow comforting, too. Her boots slid down easily, and then up again, though she had to lift her legs high for her father's steps went so far down, down into the drifts.

She plodded slowly on, towards the building where her father was saying Evensong, with only Vale the verger for company, and to make the responses.

But *I* am coming now, Fanny said, and went on alone, in the last of the afternoon light, and the deep, deep snow, to join him.

Fanny knew that very early on Christmas morning, before even she was awake, Mr Vale would come to light the big stove that stood at the back of the church. He would stoke it high, open up the flues, and pull down the grate, and stay there with it until everyone came for morning service, and the building was as warm as he could make it, as warm as it could ever be made.

Which, in mid-winter, was never very warm at all. But tonight, the stove was still dark and the church was as cold as death. It caught Fanny's breath and made her chest hurt as she breathed it in, the cold seemed to go deep, deep down into her bones and settle there.

She stood quite close to the door, and looked down the little church to where the candlelight filled the chancel, beyond the beautiful stone arch. Around the arch were carved the running bodies of animals – a hare, a fox, a rabbit, a squirrel, a badger, a stoat, chasing one another, nose to tail, endlessly. And they ran in rings around the tops of the pillars, too. The stone arch was ribbed, with the curve of another, smaller arch immediately behind, and then another after that. Framed in it, the bare chancel, the plain altar with its pale wood, and one window, dark now, but by daylight, coloured deep blue and sea-green, with at the centre a crown of gold on the head of God, who sat enthroned among angels. Fanny loved the window. Loved the whole church, its grey stone and white-washed walls, and high box pews, its coolness and plainness.

Now she went very quietly forwards and when she got a step or two down the nave, stopped again and saw that the pulpit and the step, the arch and the pillars and all the window-ledges, high up, had been decorated with swags and garlands and branches of evergreen leaves, holly, plain and glossy-dark and also the gold-edged kind, and all thick with berries. The ivy had been set in clumps and clusters, and then made to trail down the stone, and instead of mistletoe – for Father would never allow mistletoe inside the church, it was a pagan thing, he said – the ivy had been whitened here and there with flour, made into a water paste and then let dry, so that now it shone as if covered with milk-white flowers. Oh pretty, thought Fanny, the green and the white, and the red of the berries. The prettiest thing.

From within the chancel, Father's voice rose, plain, tuneful, grave. 'O Lord, save thy people.'

And Mr Vale the verger came back, sure, with the response. 'And bless thine inheritance.'

'Give peace in our time, O Lord.'

And under her breath, Fanny sang, too, almost silently, the beautiful words she had known, it seemed, since the day she was born. 'Because there is none other that fighteth for us, but only thou, O God.'

Though in her heart, she said, but *I* will fight, *I* will fight, and had a glorious vision of herself, slaying dragons and devils with the shining sword. For she was often puzzled by God, but she had never doubted for one moment the existence and power of the Devil.

But not here, not tonight. Tonight, she knew that no demon nor ghost nor evil spirit of any kind dared walk abroad.

If I look up to the roof, she thought suddenly, I shall see angels.

She moved into one of the pews and knelt down, and went on listening to her father's voice, comforted by it, and wondered and wondered about the strange story of Christmas.

'The grace of our Lord Jesus Christ, and the love of God and the fellowship of the Holy Ghost, be with us all evermore.'

29

'Amen,' said Fanny, clear out loud, and her voice rang, on the stone-cold air, so that her father half-turned his head, knowing now that she was there.

Then the candles were all snuffed out, and he came down towards her, holding the lantern that threw flickering shadows up into his face, making it look lined and darkly hollowed out around the eyes and mouth, and sending his tall outline leaping up the wall. Fanny put her hand in his, and felt the fingers stiff with the cold. 'Child, child!' he said, and chafed hers gently in his own.

They went together to the church door and opened it, and saw that now there was the full moonlight falling onto the snow, and making it gleam white as bone.

'Christmas Eve!' said Fanny. 'Christmas Eve!' Her father smiled. And they began to walk together, steadily home across the snow.

For the next few hours, she darted about like a restless bird, hopping here, skipping there, too excited, too unsettled, wanting the hours to pass quickly, yet wanting it to go on being Christmas Eve, the magic waiting time, forever.

They had tea, with cinnamon toast and raisin cake, before the fire in Mother's sewing-room, and then Father went off to his study to write the sermon for tomorrow and his Christmas letters and Mother was busy again with her secrets, and closed the drawing-room door tight, and Will was cross and only in a mood for teasing. So that in the end, Fanny wandered about by herself, upstairs and downstairs, in and out, and fretted, and thought and puzzled. And yet she was happy.

At six, Mother came out to find her, and Nancy came up from the kitchen and Will down from the nursery floor, and for the next hour, they hung the green branches all about the hall and the holly wreath up in the porch, and trailed the garlands of ivy, twined with ribbon, all the way up the banisters, and it looked as fine as it had ever looked. 'Christmas Eve,' Fanny said. And, dug out of his room to come and admire, Father stood beaming in the middle of the hall, and said, 'Christmas. Blessed Christmas!'

After that, she went upstairs, and Nancy followed with the steaming water jugs, and the tin bath was set out before the nursery fire.

'Christmas Eve,' Fanny said, and shivered, in spite of the heat of the water. 'Christmas Eve!'

Downstairs again, then, she behind Will, and her long white nightgown tickled her legs and the lambskin slippers were snug around her feet. She went slowly, stair by stair, holding back and spinning out the golden moments. The hall looked suddenly quite different in its garlands of green; a strange, new place.

The door to the drawing-room was still tight shut. Silence. Fanny stood, holding her breath. Then, from below stairs came Nancy, and Kate the scullery maid, in best black and without their aprons, hair scraped back, faces solemn, strangers all at once.

On the wall, the gas jet spurted and the flame flared within the brackets, the holly and ivy were dark and gleaming softly.

And then, oh then, the double doors were flung open, and there in the long drawing-room, beyond the lamps and the flames of the fire, the Christmas tree, tall as a steeple, and covered with candles like stars, with holly berries and with little oranges, that were stuck about with cloves and hung upon scarlet ribbon. Fanny thought she might faint quite away with the joy of it, and she touched her hand quickly to her breast in a moment of fear that her heart had actually stopped.

Then, quietly, in they went, to where Mother stood smiling, and Father, too.

'Oh beautiful,' said Fanny, and gazed and gazed at the tree in its glory. 'Oh beautiful.'

They sat around the fire, Fanny on the low stool, with Father in the wing chair, and Nancy and Kate just a little outside the circle, stiff and straight-backed, and the logs blazed up bravely, banked to the back of the grate, and the applewood smoke smelled sweet as sweet.

'And it came to pass in those days, that there went out a decree from Caesar Augustus, that all the world should be taxed. And all went to be taxed, every one into his own city. And Joseph also went up from Galilee, out of the city of Nazareth, into Judæa, unto the city of David, which is called Bethlehem. To be taxed with Mary his espoused wife, being great with child.'

And silently to herself, Fanny said the words as her father read them, and they sounded as beautiful as music to her, and just as strange, too, simple, yet infinitely difficult, as close and familiar to her as her own name, and yet far remote.

'And she brought forth her firstborn son, and wrapped him in swaddling clothes, and laid him in a manger; because there was no room for them in the inn.'

And the brightness and the warmth from the fire, and the blaze of the candles from the Christmas tree, danced in front of Fanny's eyes, and the room seemed to be filled with a great blaze of light, as if it were one of the rooms of heaven, and Fanny's limbs felt leaden with sleep, and her head light as a dandelion clock that might be blown away, puff, from its stalk and float, float, off on the air.

'But Mary kept all these things, and pondered them in her heart.'

Yes, thought Fanny, oh yes. And then listened to the silence that fell suddenly on the room as her father finished the reading.

She scarcely remembered going upstairs to bed at all, there was just a blur of faces and voices, firelight and candlelight, and the sensation of her own tiredness. The stairs to the top of the house had never seemed so many.

She awoke, quite suddenly, and lay, not moving, for several moments, wondering what sound she could have heard, what might have disturbed her. Then, she thought that she *did* hear a sound, very faint, not from within the house, but from somewhere outside and far away.

Fanny listened and listened. Nothing. Silence. She slipped out of bed and went to the window, and shivered, for the room was very cold.

When she drew back the curtains, she looked down on a magic world, gleaming white under the moon, with every line of the church roof and the church tower, gravestone and tree and hedge and wall, softened and blurred. The moonlight was very bright, and the sky was thick, thick with stars, glittering like pin points. For a few seconds she stood, stock still there, looking, looking, and feeling the strange feeling that she might be entirely alone, the only one left alive in that cold, quiet, beautiful world.

Then, from a distance away, again she heard something, a voice perhaps, coming on the wind and, looking beyond, past the church to the fields, she saw them, a line of lights, like stars or glow-worms, or fireflies, bobbing about, drawing very gradually nearer. She pushed open her window, so that its edging braid of snow toppled and fell, far down, and a little of it puffed back into the room, and drifted to the floor.

The air smelled sharply of frost. Fanny leaned out a little way, and felt it so cold it burned the skin of her face.

And then, she heard their voices much more clearly, a word or two passed down the procession now and then, and the lanterns, held high, came steadily nearer, until soon she could distinguish them more clearly, though they were all muffled up in greatcoats and leggings, boots and scarves and caps, against the cold.

'The carol singers are come!' Will said in a low voice, but still it made her start. He was standing in the doorway in his nightshirt. Fanny could see his eyes round with excitement.

'They've come, Fanny,' and he moved to stand beside her at the window, and watch as they made their slow way towards the Rectory through the deep drifted snow, ten or a dozen of them, men and boys, all from the village and round about, and carrying their instruments under their arms, or across their bodies, and every one with his own lantern, though they could not have needed them in the bright moonlight, except for decoration.

'Come on, Fanny,' for the singers were making their way around to the front of the house. She took Will's hand and crept out and down the passage, and into the small box-room that was scarcely used. Here the old baby crib was stored, and Father's trunk, lettered in black with his initials, and a strange case full of stuffed fish with glassy eyes, that Fanny hated.

Now, it was Will's turn to push up the window, and difficult, the sash was hardly ever lifted, and very stiff. By the time he had managed it, the carol singers were tuning their instruments, a note floating up now and again, from fiddle, or clarionet or pipe.

Then, Seth Locke, the senior of them and leader, called for order and quiet, and gave the note and, suddenly, it began, the old tune came up to them through the clear cold air and, closing her eyes, Fanny was transported by it, and clutched Will's hand and squeezed it tight for sheer joy. And Will did not snatch it back to himself quite straight away.

> *Joseph was an old man*
> *An old man was he*
> *When first he courted Mary*
> *What a virgin was she.*
>
> *Joseph and Mary*
> *Walked out in Garden's wood*
> *Were apples, plums and cherries*
> *As red as they grow.*

They were deep voices, the voices of older boys and grown men, and the instruments were the homely ones, not harps and dulcimers, and golden trumpets. Yet Fanny thought that they must surely be angels that sang and played, and she herself already, and quite certainly, in heaven.

When they reached the end of the long carol, they paused before striking up with another, and after that, they saw the bright beam of light fall across the snow as the front door was opened, and heard Father's voice, calling them to come in, and there was much stamping and bumping and banging of feet. Fanny and Will crept down inch by careful inch, so as not to make the stair boards creak, and sat on the step, high above the hall. And listened again as the men sang the Wassail, and Richard the Carrier gave them a merry Christmas. After that, laughter, and the smell of hot pies, and the chink of the tankards of mulled ale as the tray went round.

Peering through the banisters, Fanny could just see the tops of their heads, and a glimpse of Father's arm, and the garlands of greenery all around. And if her mother, glancing up, caught sight of her, if she did, she looked away very quickly, and moved back a little, and did not say or do anything about it at all.

The carol singers gave one more verse, and then they were going, calling goodnight and wishing a happy Christmas over and over again, and Will touched her hand to go back upstairs.

I am not tired at all, Fanny thought. I shall never go to sleep now, for now it is almost Christmas.

And lay in her bed in the white moonlight, eyes wide, straining her ears for the last faint voices of the carol singers coming back to her across the snowy fields.

Now, it is almost Christmas, Fanny said.

And slept.

CHRISTMAS DAY

OH, THE JOY of waking, and remembering at once that it was Christmas morning. It was still only half-light, but because of the white radiance of the snow there was a brightness in her room, and Fanny could see perfectly well. She scrambled from her bed, and ran to the window and looked outside, but she could see nothing for the ferns and whorls and delicate tracery of rime on the inside of the pane. She touched her finger to it and it burned with the cold, and the air was cold, too, so that she dived back at once into her bed.

And then, oh the joy of seeing the stocking hung on the bedstead knob and the bumps and bundles pushing out in all directions; and the pleasure of pulling out first this and then that, very gradually, carefully, heart racing with excitement, of looking and feeling and stroking and squeezing and guessing – of finding, finding a book, full of wonderful coloured castles and silvery towers, and mythical monsters and princes and princesses, elves and goblins, winged beasts, fiery

dragons; of finding a rainbow of wax pencils and a
frieze of dolls made out of card, with clothes for them
made of paper; finding sheets of scrap pictures of
cherubs, and a wooden top that spun in a glorious arc of
colour when she twirled it between her fingers; and a
very small wooden horse, with real hair for its mane
and tail, and the packet of comfits wrapped in golden
paper and the red apple and the orange, orange
tangerine, and the handful of warm brown nuts.

Fanny laid out her presents in a row upon the counterpane, and touched, and gazed, opened the book, and
closed it again, stroked the mane and tail of the little
horse. Then she heard Will come, bumping and banging along, with his hands full of ships and soldiers and a
jointed clown on a string that you jerked, and a slab of
butterscotch. Oh, the joy of its being Christmas! Of
tumbling down the stairs to venison pie for breakfast,
and real yellow cream on the bowls of porridge.

Then Father went ahead on his own to the church,
and there was all the dressing in best coat and bonnet,
and after she was quite ready, or so she thought, her
mother went quickly away, and came back from her
little sewing-room with a brown paper parcel.

'A happy Christmas, little Fanny.' Inside, the most
perfect, grey fur muff on a shining, silver-grey cord –
made out of a collar Mother had had on a coat worn
before she was married.

Fanny put the cord of the muff carefully round her
neck and slipped her hands into either end. It was like
being close to the warm body of some still-alive creature,
and her fingers met there and clasped together tight.

They were to walk, not across the churchyard from the

back door, but out at the front and around the path, as was only proper as the Rectory family, on Sundays and festival days. The snow crunched under their feet, and everywhere, the sun caught on a million beads and drops of hoar frost and threw off a million tiny rainbows, intensely bright and glittering. On the gate hung a spider's web, infinitely delicate, and stiff as frozen lace, with the spider itself frozen into the heart of it. And on the hedges and trees, and fences and posts, were the seams of snow. By the lych-gate, there was a robin on a yew branch, and in the way of robins, it kept company beside them, hop-hop, half a yard away over the snow, its breast red as a soldier's coat, its eye bead-bright.

And there was everyone else coming to church, and the carriage bearing m'lord and m'lady, with the poor horses slithering and sliding on the frozen road; and old people walking very gingerly, and children skipping, and breath pluming out, white as woodsmoke, on the cold, cold air.

And 'A happy Christmas to you! Oh, a happy Christmas!'

Inside the church, the stove roared and blazed but it still felt bitter chill, and they could not sit close to the warmth either, the Rectory pew was right at the front. Fanny tucked her hands deep into her muff and moved closer to Mother and then stuck out her legs, to admire the shine of her black button boots, and held the muff rather high, so that it might be seen. And Will, so proud in his best, stiff collar, would not catch her eye.

Father's sermon was about the real love and peace of Christmas. 'Peace in your homes. Peace in your hearts.' But privately, Fanny thought peace a very dull thing, and her mind wandered away from Father's words, and she puzzled again about God, and whether, if she turned her head very quickly, and without any warning, she might catch a glimpse of Him, before He ducked out of sight.

O come ye, O come ye to Bethlehem,
Come and behold Him,
Born the King of Angels . . .

Oh yes, angels, oh, angels. That was all right again. She was quite at home with angels.

As always, she felt suddenly shy, standing by outside the church porch at the end of the service, while Father gave greetings to everyone, and being stiff in her best clothes, all unlike herself. But then, a great joy spurted through her as she looked around, at the beauty of the white snow, with its sheen of frost gleaming so bright under the morning sun that it hurt her eyes, and at red cheeks and bright eyes, at smart bonnets and cheerful faces, so that she wanted to dance and sing and shout, 'Oh glory, glory!'

Until she looked across the churchyard at the gravestones that leaned this way and that, and at the grey stone marking the place where her brothers lay – Edmund Charles and Arthur Frederick. And a picture came into her head, of them lying small and stiff and infinitely cold under the piled-up earth and snow, and of all the sleepers buried here, dead, so long, long dead. It troubled her, she wanted to question it, and for a few moments a shadow touched her, and she felt far away from all the people talking together, smiling, nodding, wishing a merry Christmas.

After that though, the going home, and Will made a snowball and threw it at her back – but only gently, and when Mother spoke to him, it was not very sharply so that he only went on grinning. And they reached the house in time for everyone else arriving – the curate, who had been taking the early service out at Sawley, five miles away, and his new, new, smiling wife, and Uncle Jack, Mother's bachelor brother. And in half an hour, Sam Hay came over from Highwood Starrup, in the pony trap, with Grandmother Fairfax wrapped in rugs.

And then the Christmas table, with its snow-white cloth and polished glasses winking in the light, and the handsome, best silver that made Fanny clap her hands and laugh. And on the sideboard, a white dish on its stand was piled high with fruit, green and gold, purple and orange, yellow and red, and another held nuts, and a third sweetmeats, sugared almonds and egg-yellow marchpane, and jellies covered in sugar crystal. Then they all sat down and the food came, smelling of richness and savoury juices, and steaming hot.

The skin of the roasted fowl was crinkled and golden brown, the gravy ran like a thick, dark river; potatoes were fluffed up in the dish like mountains of snow. Fanny felt her mouth pucker up with hunger as Father said the grace and carved the bird and poured out the glasses of purple-red wine.

Then Fanny caught Father's eye and he smiled at her, so sweet, so tenderly loving, so happy a smile, that she thought she might melt all away with happiness.

'Christmas,' she said abruptly, out loud, 'oh, it *is* Christmas!'

And everyone laughed.

43

When the pudding was borne in, its dark, moist, gleaming roundness licked about by the blue flame where Nancy had set the brandy alight just as she stepped in, they all gave a cheer, and Will even banged the back of his spoon upon the table, until he saw Mother's quick frown. Fanny crumbled up her slice very carefully, moving it about the plate until she found the shining threepenny piece and the tiny silver horseshoe; and the curate got the wedding bells, and Uncle Jack the bachelor button, and Will got the donkey, and turned red, and everyone laughed again. And in the middle of the laughter, the door opened and Nancy came in, all anxious, and Mother looked quickly across at Father.

'They have found Seth Locke collapsed in the snow. They have carried him to his cottage,' Father said gravely. And stood up. 'I am sent for,' and he went out, touching Mother's arm gently, on the way.

'Of course he must go,' she said to them around the table, but for a time, they were all silent, eating quietly, and not liking to go back to being jolly, and Fanny's heart blazed inside her with rage, that God should have let Seth Locke be ill, and take Father away from the Christmas table. She wished that they were a different kind of family, undisturbed by such things. But at once, she bowed her head for shame, and thought only of the poor old man lying sick and cold in the snow, and was glad, glad that Father was such a man, and to be proud of.

After a time, Will spoke up and told them a very silly, funny joke about a donkey so that Mother would know he had not really minded about getting it after all, and then the curate took up, and told a silly, funny story –

though not as funny as Will's, funny though – about two cross-eyed pigs, and when she looked across the table, she saw that Grandmother Fairfax had gone peacefully to sleep over her plate of fruit and nuts, and she caught Will's eye, and Will gave her a great wink.

So the meal was not altogether spoiled, and afterwards they went into the drawing-room, and had their stocking presents down to play with. Fanny went, with her dressing-doll, behind the big sofa and sat on the floor with her back to it, looking out of the tall windows onto the front drive, so that she would be able to see her father return. They would wait to open the gifts that were under the tree, Mother said, until they were all together again.

And so the time passed, but very slowly, and Fanny fell into a kind of trance, watching the dazzling snow and a blackbird that was hop-hopping about very close to the windows, looking for food, and now and then the branches of the fir tree trembled as a slight breeze passed through them, and dropped little pats of snow down with a plop and a flurry.

All at once, Fanny realised that her mother had come to stand near to her, and then she bent down and took hold of Fanny's hand and smiled.

'When will Father come back?'

'He will stay as long as he is needed.'

'Yes.'

And her mother came and pulled over the low stool and sat companionably down beside her, then, and took up the doll. And they stayed together, admiring the paper clothes, the fur-trimmed cloak and bonnet, the lacy dinner gown, and the great brimmed hat,

45

covered in flowers and swathed with net, that Fanny could fit onto the doll as she wanted, with tabs, and Mother helped her to change the outfits and they both laughed a good deal. Behind them, Will and Uncle Jack and the curate argued and contradicted one another over the way the rigging should be threaded on a wooden ship, and Grandmother Fairfax told a long, long tale of India to the curate's smiling wife.

And then, suddenly, the banging and scraping of boots in the porch, and the front door opening, and Father was back.

Fanny got up and ran to him. And then stopped short, seeing his serious face, and she knew. And her mother glanced at him, and knew, too. 'Oh,' said Fanny softly, '*Oh!*' and felt tears of rage, rage and bewilderment and sorrow, for it was Christmas Day, it was Christmas Day, and nothing should be allowed to happen to spoil that. But it had.

'Seth Locke has died,' she said out loud. Her father looked hard at her for a moment or two, then beckoned her to him as he went to sit in the wing chair close to the fire, and warm himself. Fanny stood stiffly, mutinous. '*Why* does God make people die? Why, *why*, Father?'

There was a silence in the bright room.

Fanny had loved Seth Locke. He had had not a single hair on his head, and only one or two teeth left in his mouth, and a skin like the surface of a cobnut, and thick arms like great tree roots, and he had often lifted Fanny up, to sit on the back of one of the farm horses, and even though he seemed old, he'd swung her up as if she weighed less than half an ounce to him.

'I sat with him,' her father said quietly. 'He was

46

asleep and awake, very fitfully. In much pain. They had laid him on the settle, close to the stove. But he was very cold. I found blankets and a coat to cover him, but he was still cold. Then his eyes closed and he didn't move. I could barely see his breath. I wondered . . . I knew it was not to be long.'

Everyone in the room was still, Will and Uncle Jack at the table, and the curate beside his wife, and Grandmother Fairfax in the upright chair, with Mother standing behind her. And Fanny close beside her father, taut as a bow. Everyone listened.

'And then, quite suddenly, he opened his eyes,' Father said. 'He opened his eyes wide, and he sat upright easily, without any pain, and he gripped hold of my hand.' He paused for a long time, and Fanny saw that his eyes had filled with tears, and his face was solemn with the memory of what had happened, solemn, and strangely joyful, too, for all that he wept.

'He said in a bold voice to me, "I have seen the glory," and then again, "I have seen the glory." And he laid his head back on the pillow. And he was dead.'

Father looked around, from one to another, until at last his eyes rested upon Fanny.

'Thanks be to God,' he said.

And there was not a sound in the room except the spark and crackle of the fire. Until the curate said, 'Amen.'

Then her father reached out his arm and drew Fanny to him. 'And there was not only a death today, little Fanny, there was a birth, too, a baby born for Christmas.'

I know, I know all about that, she wanted to say tearfully, all about the Christ child and the shepherds in the fields and glory to God in the highest, but Seth Locke has still died, and never, never will lead the carols again.

But then her father said, 'Thomas Tumney's wife was delivered of a son, early this morning. I met some of the older children in the lane, sliding on the ice.' He looked at Fanny. 'A death and a new life.'

Fanny did not answer.

'I must get together a basket of food for them,' her mother said. 'The Tumneys have little enough, heaven knows.' For there were ten Tumneys, the new boy would make eleven children, and Thomas Tumney always ill since he fell off the hayrick three years before and could not work; they were the poorest of the poor.

'Shall we go and see the baby, then? May I go? May we go now, today, at once?' But her mother frowned at Fanny to be quiet, and she saw that Father was suddenly weary, resting back in his chair. And at that moment, Nancy came in with the tea-tray, and Grandmother woke with a start, and Will knocked the fire-irons over into the hearth with a great clang-clatter, and soon, soon, they would have the gifts from the tree.

'For it is still Christmas,' Fanny said to herself. 'It is still the very middle of Christmas.'

It was not until much later, when she was gazing at the candles, freshly lit and blazing again on the tree, and the beautiful little sewing case was in her hands, with its silver thimble and little pair of silver scissors, all her own, it was not until that perfect moment that she remembered.

Father had told them of Seth Locke's last words, and of the birth of the new baby. But he had not answered her question.

ST STEPHEN'S DAY

'THE BABY,' Fanny said the moment she came into the dining-room at breakfast time on the morning after Christmas Day. 'I am going with Father, to see the Tumneys' new baby.'

Brother Will made a scornful, boy's face, and blew onto his spoonful of hot porridge with a loud noise, but bent his head down to eat quite quietly as their mother came in, and that made Fanny angry. She loved her brother, he was her best, her dearest friend, and every now and then, she hated him.

'Mama, *when* will Father take me to see the new baby? When shall we start out?'

But just at that moment her father opened the door and came in.

'*When* shall we go, please can it be at once, straight away after breakfast?'

Oh, the anguish of waiting, for her father only frowned very slightly, and said his grace, and sat down and watched Mother pour out his tea, sprinkled sugar very carefully over his porridge, and did not speak a single word. And brother Will kicked her shin beneath the tablecloth, but would not look at her, only away, out of the window, smiling a secret smile.

It is over, Fanny thought, Christmas is all done with and everyone is cross, the bright lights have been put out and there is nothing but the days and days and days of January to come. And she felt a terrible grey disappointment settle over and around her, and a lump in her heart, cold and heavy, as if it were a stone, and she stared down into her bowl, stirring and stirring the mealy lumps of pale porridge, no longer a bit hungry.

'Fanny is a crosspatch, Fanny has a black dog,' Will said, and then again, twice, in a sing-song. 'Fanny is a crosspatch, Fanny has a . . .' and Fanny felt her eyes prick with sudden sharp tears.

But then, looking up, she saw that Father's face was dark as thunder, and suddenly Will was silent and quite still and even seemed to be shrinking down inside his jacket. For Father's rage, if it ever broke, was to be feared.

After a moment, he turned his glance away from Will, to her.

'It is cold, Fanny,' he said, 'bitterly, bitterly cold. But the sun is shining and the sky is as blue as a blackbird's egg and quite without the smallest cloud, and the branches of the trees are lacey-white.'

And he cut his triangle of toast into a smaller triangle, very neatly and carefully. Fanny watched him, and waited, waited.

'And today is the feast of St Stephen. The day after Christmas Day.'

And he ate a very small corner of the toast, chewing very slowly, and swallowing, and then taking a drink of his tea, and swallowing that, before speaking again. But this time, when he looked across the table at Fanny, she saw that his eyes were smiling and his mouth was just beginning to smile, too.

'And I am a busy parson, in charge of a church and a wide parish, and today is a working day, Christmas or no Christmas.'

And he reached over and chose an apple from the glass bowl of fruit, his hand hovering above this one and that one, before deciding, and taking the one nearest to him, and putting it on his plate and picking up the knife.

Then, his eyes were laughing, his whole face was crinkled with teasing laughter, and Fanny felt a great spurt of love for him.

'So that after I have eaten every morsel of my breakfast, little Fanny, I have to work. I must go out visiting. There is a poor widow to be consoled, and a very large family with a very new baby, to be cheered.'

Fanny could hardly keep still on her chair for excitement but she sat on her hands, and pinched herself, and waited and, glancing sideways, saw that brother Will was scowling into his plate, with his dark eyebrows drawn tight together.

'I should very much like,' Father said, wiping his mouth upon his napkin, 'to have my daughter go with me for company. And the poor widow of Seth Locke and the poor wife of Thomas Tumney, and all the Tumney children, and most especially the brand new Tumney baby, would very much like to have her, too.'

53

And he stood up, seeming very tall and straight. 'Well, child?'

'Yes, oh yes? Yes, Father?'

'Are you going to keep us all waiting?'

Fanny jumped off her chair, so that she knocked it over. 'Shall we go now? This morning, at once? Are we going already?'

'This very moment.' And he clapped his hands to shoo her away; though she needed no shooing, was out of the room and across the hall and up the stairs. But as she went, she glanced over her shoulder, to see that Father had stayed behind in the dining-room, to speak to Will, and because she was overflowing with happiness, she said, 'Don't be angry' to him, under her breath, and willed the message to fly back and reach her father. 'He didn't mean harm, oh, don't, don't be angry.'

For it *is* still Christmas, she said, leaping up the stairs to her own room, to dress herself for the bitter cold morning, and the long walk to the village. It *is* still Christmas, after all.

When they stepped out of the front door, Fanny caught her breath with the shock of the most intense cold she had ever felt, and with wonder, too, at the beauty that she saw before her.

The world sparkled. The surface of the snow had frozen hard, and it shone like a faceted mirror, glinted and gleamed in the bright sunshine and the clear, cold air. As they began to walk, their feet made a ringing sound on the hard frozen ground, where a narrow path had been cleared down the drive, through the deep snow.

'Oh, beautiful,' Fanny said, and held firmly onto her father's hand, letting her feet slide a little, this way and that. 'Oh, beautiful.'

And beside her, beneath the great cedar tree, she saw the blackbird, hop-hopping, as if it were on a spring, over the snow. And its eye, ringed around with an orange-gold rim, watched her.

After that, neither she nor her father spoke again for a long while, because once they had left the Rectory drive and reached the lane, the snow, although it had been packed down in places, was still very deep, and walking through it was hard work. They had no breath left for talking. And the basket that Fanny was holding, which her mother had packed with good things for the Tumneys, was straight away too heavy for her, and she had to give it up for her father to carry.

They went very steadily down the lane that led between the high banks where in spring the primroses were thick and butter-coloured, and cowslips and hundreds of white and purple violets grew, and on either side the hawthorn hedges were interspersed with trees, bare and severe and stately against the blue sky.

The air smelled of fresh, sweet coldness, and of snow too, though Fanny did not really understand how, for when she picked up a handful and brought it close to her nose, it smelled simply of nothing at all.

At the end of the lane, the stream emerged from between the banks, deep down in the ditch; Fanny peered and saw that it was opaque and frozen completely stiff. She wondered whether it had been like a living person, walking along quietly but gradually being slowed and slowed, as their blood ran thicker, more sluggishly, colder, through the veins, until at last, they could hardly move – and then, did not move at all; or whether, one moment the water had been rippling over the stones, flowing fast, as it always did, and the next, it had been seized by the cold and stopped dead in its tracks, so that somehow all the movement and light and liquidity was crystallised and held fast in the grip of the frost, exactly as it had been when moving, only suddenly *not* moving, but stiff and still.

She dropped Father's hand and went closer to the bank. On either side, the grasses and the thick dead stalks of hogweed and cow parsley were powdery white and stiff, like sugar sticks. Closer to the water, whitened clumps of bog roses and mats of moss; higher up, the scrub and bracken arched up on itself, to form a roof, all pierced and torn through with holes.

Her father had stopped and was waiting for her, but Fanny did not move, only bent down, to where, on the grass, she saw a shrew. Its fur was frozen and its small, pointed face, with the long corkscrew snout, was frozen, too. In a moment of living, it had been taken by death, of cold. She picked up the body and held it in the palm of her hand. Its tail was thin and stiff.

And down in the ditch, and in all the hedgerow bottoms, she thought, how many other tiny creatures lay, frozen to death? And birds, wrens and tits, packed together in tree-holes and under the eaves of privies, the smallest, frailest birds, unable to find any food or water.

She stood still in the bright, bitter morning, holding the shrew, until at last her father came back to her, and took the tiny creature and laid it gently down again between the clumps of frozen grass.

At the end of the lane, the ways forked, right to the open country that led up onto Ladyman Barrow. When they reached there, Fanny looked across to where it lay, white and softened now, merging gently into the other pillowed hills and fields around. Once the snow had melted, it would be brown again, dark, shadowed, even when the high summer sun shone full at the middle of the day.

Fanny loved, and was afraid of the Barrow, afraid of its bareness and openness to the wide sky, the strange sounds that were all about it, the way the wind keened there and the hawks and buzzards swooped and soared and then plunged suddenly down, and the way the shadows came behind and up and over to engulf you in abrupt chill greyness and make you imagine dreadful things. There were no trees, nothing to break the wide, bare brownness. But in summer, it was beautiful. The sun baked the earth, and made the furze give up a rich, pungent, herby smell, and the ground felt hot to your hand. She and Will were allowed out on the Barrow just so far, to where the white wooden signpost marked the crossing of all the ways. Then they would run off the dusty tracks, and plunge into the scrub and lie on their backs in the sun, while the butterflies fluttered all about their heads and over their faces, and you could reach out a hand and wait, very still, for one to come to rest on it, and tremble there, opening and closing its wings.

She loved the sandy-brown and buff rabbits that bumped ahead of them, before diving into their hundreds of holes. And once even there had been a snake, basking in the sun, its skin iridescent, its eye evil-bright. Will had poked it gently with the tip of a stick and it had uncoiled itself, fast as lightning, and slithered away and vanished.

Last year, they had found the remains of an old stone shelter, a cairn built by some heath-dweller or furze-cutter, long ago. Inside was only the bare earth for a floor; in the corner, an opening in the roof above a rough hearth where a few turves, crumbling and blackened, still remained. Fanny had picked up a fragment, and smelled its faint, charred, acrid smell. Then, she had made a broom out of some brushy furze, and swept the hut out.

'We could live here,' Will had said. 'We could keep ponies and ride all day on the Barrow, and sleep on the ground at night in front of the dying embers, like gypsy-people.'

And Fanny had been ready to, at once. But then, a storm had blown up; low cloud shrouded the Barrow in a wet mist that clung to their hair and clothes like cobwebs, and then a wind had driven the rain in through the doorway and the window spaces, and down the chimney hole, soaking it all and churning the floor to mud. Then it had seemed a lonely, little, miserable place.

'Poor person who lived there,' Fanny had thought as they ran and ran through the rain, for home.

The left-hand fork of the lane led towards the village, and here the snow had drifted higher than ever to one side, so that she and Father had to keep in file, close to the opposite stone wall, and Fanny's boots sank deep into the soft, cold drifts almost to their tops. But she felt bold and important, coming visiting with her father, and when first one and then another person saw them, and stopped to talk, she felt proud, too. She was there because Father had wanted her, for her company and because he felt that others would welcome her also.

Seth Locke's cottage was at the far end of the village street, beyond the pond and the horse trough, the inn and Ellen Rose's post office. It was one of three that were joined in a row together, and set back beyond a long, straight path that led up through the middle of the garden.

In summer, there were rows of giant hollyhocks on either side, with floppy petals all coloured pale, like clothes that had faded from too many washings, Fanny thought. And in between the hollyhocks and sweet williams, the columbines and cornflowers and the net of small, frilled pinks, were set creamy cauliflowers and purple cabbages, because Seth Locke had liked them there. They were as good as any proper flower, he had once told Fanny. That same day, he had picked her a little nosegay and surrounded it with cool damp primula leaves, and she had felt like a princess, carrying it carefully home.

Now she walked solemnly up the same path, whose small uneven bricks were treacherous with hard-packed snow, and looked at the billows of it piled over the earth of the garden, and thought of everything that had been growing and living buried deep and cold, and of poor Seth Locke himself, who was dead too and would never see his garden growing again.

59

Before they reached the cottage door, it had opened, and there was Seth Locke's daughter Flora, come across the winter fields from her own home seven miles away at Nune Abbas. And seeing her, with the dark cottage room behind her, Fanny felt suddenly over-awed, and nervous too, so that she touched her father's hand for a second before drawing herself up, very tall and straight, anxious to do everything in just the right way.

Seth Locke's wife Mary was sitting on the settle beside the fire, which was banked high and darkly smoking, not giving any warmth or brightness out into the cramped room.

Her face, when Fanny could make it out more clearly, was pasty and pinched with sorrow, and her eyes looked sore. She had on a best, shiny black dress with a long row of buttons, and bands of plain tucks down the front, and a clean apron over, and her hair was coiled round and round, tight as a bread plait at the back of her head.

Fanny stayed near to the door while her father went in and took Mary Locke's hand and held it, speaking to her quietly. She had scarcely ever been inside the cottage. Whenever she had visited Seth Locke, he had been outside in the garden, or the lane, in the yard behind the smithy, or on the road, leading one of the farm horses. Seth Locke hadn't been a man for indoors.

She started, realising that her father was looking across at her, and then went forwards slowly, and stood beside him. Close to, Mary Locke's face looked sadder than ever, her eyes watery but as though they were looking far away, and she knitted her fingers together in her lap.

Fanny felt her mouth go dry, and she licked her lips and swallowed. But then, thinking about how it was, remembering how Father had come home yesterday to the Christmas family, and told them of Seth Locke's dying, remembering Seth himself, and how she had liked him, Fanny bent down, and put her arms around Mary Locke, and hugged her as tight as she could, smelling the cupboard smell of the best black shiny dress.

'Oh,' she said, and looked up into her face, 'oh, I am truly sorry that Seth Locke has died, but I am truly glad that he had seen the glory.'

And for quite a long time, she stayed, holding tight to the woman's hand, wanting to be a comfort to her.

Then, from behind, in the doorway, Flora Locke said, 'Would you step up now, and see him?'

There was a silence until Fanny stood resolutely up, and looked at her father and at Flora Locke.

'I will go,' she said in a clear voice. 'Thank you, I will go up and see him.'

'It is only to say goodbye, Fanny. *I* must, but you . . .'

'Yes,' Fanny said, wanting to and not wanting to, but quite certain what she must do. 'I will go with you.'

Her father smiled at her and touched her shoulder, and then they followed behind Mary Locke, and her daughter, slowly, slowly up the steep little twisting staircase, and into the bedroom above. Here, there was a bright white light from the reflection of the snow on the roof outside the high window, and Fanny saw that a great swag of snow hung down like a bee-swarm from the thatch, and attached to it were silken, transparent icicles, thick as reeds.

The bedroom was cold as cold, and very neat, with rag mats on the boarded floor. As they went in, Father seemed as tall as a tree, and had to bend so as not to hit his head on the beam. Fanny shut her eyes tightly for a second, and drew in a breath from deep down in her stomach, up and up through her whole body.

When she opened her eyes again, she was looking at the high brass bed that filled one end of the room, and at Seth Locke who lay there, pale as pale in the white light, on the white pillow, under the white, white sheet.

Behind her, Mary Locke gave a little sob and a sniff, but then, composing herself, went to stand beside Father while he said a prayer and gave them a blessing. And in the cold, cold room, Fanny began to shiver, and pressed her knees together and her elbows close in to her body and, hearing her father's voice, low and steady, thought suddenly, 'I shall remember this. I shall always remember.'

Then she stepped forwards, two, three small steps, and reached out her hand, and touched the folded hands of the dead man, and looked full into his calm face, so like it had always been to her, and yet so utterly strange.

'Goodbye, Seth Locke,' Fanny said to him in a whisper.

And his hand was as cold as the coldest stone to her warm touch.

Although the Lockes' cottage had been dark downstairs, and crowded with heavy furniture, it had still felt strangely empty to Fanny, because of the death; and even when the four of them sat down and drank tea and ate small slices of plain seed cake, she felt there were dark corners full of emptiness all around.

Thomas Tumney's cottage was no bigger, it was a damp, dark little place, close to the pond, and set up against a high bank that dripped dank growth and creeper, and the front door opened straight onto the street.

But inside, there seemed to be not a single nook or cranny left vacant, every corner was crammed with children, while the range, a great settle, a laden clothes horse and Thomas Tumney's couch, for he had not been able to go up the stairs since the injury to his back, took up the rest of the room. It was very hot as the fire in the range glowed red, and the room smelled of damp washing and children's bodies, and boiling bones, and the wet hair of the scruffy dog which lay on the rug. In the midst of it all, on the low stool, sat Thomas Tumney's wife, her hair springing out from its knot and standing up wildly all about her head; and beside her, in the low wooden crib, swaddled in old pieces of sheeting, the baby, born on Christmas Day.

As they went in, Fanny felt eyes watching her from every corner of the room, and, half-glancing round, saw faces peering out from behind the furniture. When they had come walking down the street towards the cottage, Tumney children had come out to meet them, inquisitive, large-eyed but silent.

Fanny stood, feeling out of place and uncomfortable, but when her father looked at her, she went up to Tumney's wife, and set down the basket which they

63

had brought, full of Christmas food and, below that, a layer of clothes for the baby, while on the very top, a crusty loaf of Nancy's bread, new baked that morning and wrapped in a cloth.

At once, the Tumney children came closer, to peer down into the basket, and lift the corner of the cloth, trying to see what was inside and, at the same time, staring at Fanny. They all looked very like one another except that some had red hair, like their mother, and others were dark, and they were dressed all anyhow in clothes that did not fit or belong. And Fanny felt suddenly angry, that Thomas Tumney could not work, and so they had to be poor and wait for other people to bring them clothes and food, and ashamed that she had so much, clothes that were warm and bright and properly fitting to her and rooms that were full of space in which to be.

I shall remember this, too, she thought, remember the hot, crowded room and the smell of so many children and of the wet dog and the boiling bones, and the sadness on Thomas Tumney's face, lying on his couch.

Then one of the older children, the girl Eliza whom Fanny sat near to in the schoolroom, came up to the crib, and bent down, and gently lifted up the baby. She cradled him close for a moment, before moving back the clothes to show his face. And Fanny saw Eliza smile, with love and pride, and looked at the others who came crowding round, one to hold a finger, the other to touch the baby's face; she saw their gladness, the warmth of their welcome to him, and felt suddenly shy, standing outside their loving circle, until Eliza said, 'Would you not like to hold our Christian?' and proffered the baby until Fanny took him very carefully, uncertain exactly what to do.

'Put a hand here – and crook your arm so – there, there!'

'Oh,' Fanny said, and looked down into the small, delicate face, and wondered at it, at the faint violet-blue of the creased eyelid, and the rose-red of the pursed mouth, and the fine down of hair, red-gold in the light.

She put out a finger, and touched the baby's hand, and at once the small fingers curled in and gripped her own, and inside the palm, it felt sweetly damp and warm.

Fanny looked up, and saw her father watching her from the chair he had drawn up to Thomas Tumney's couch, and she smiled at him, and at Thomas, and his wife, and the faces of all the children surrounding her.

'He is so beautiful,' she said, and looked down at the baby again. 'He is beautiful.'

And for that moment, she did not feel sad nor sorry for them, only gladness, and a great, great envy.

She handed Christian back then, and sat down on a stool and, for a long time after that, she had to wait for Father, patiently, while he sat and listened, first to Thomas Tumney, and then to his wife, heard all their worries and fears, and then the story of their eldest daughter Rose, who was fourteen, and in service at Hestone Manor eleven miles away. How Rose had been ill all that winter, with fever and a cold on her chest, and how she had grown too thin and could not stop coughing all the nights, but was forced to sleep in an attic where the windows did not fit, so that the rain and wind and now the snow came in, and had to get up at five every morning to light the fires, and work in the dank scullery all day. And how two of her brothers had trudged through the deep snow on Christmas afternoon, to take her a gift and tell her about the new baby, for she had not been allowed any time off to come home herself.

When they got there, they had waited nearly a whole hour by the stable clock until, at last, Rose had come out to see them, though only for a few moments, and they had been frightened, she had looked so thin and pale and had coughed so badly. She had not been allowed even to take them into the back kitchen so they had all stood in the cold wind until she was called back for there was a big party of folk at the house for Christmas and she said everyone was needed to work. So Josh and Jonah had had to walk back home again without any food or a drink given.

'And that was Christmas Day,' said Thomas Tumney's wife, in a low, sad voice. 'And they all Christian people.'

And, of course, Father had said that he would go there himself, the very next day, and see Rose, and fetch her to the doctor, and speak to the people at the Manor, about her being kept warm, and looked after properly, and his voice had been cold and hard with anger.

After that, Thomas Tumney had begun to talk again, telling a long tale of woe and misery. And all at once, the children were shooed outside, and they urged Fanny to go with them, and they made snowballs and slid about in the lane, and went to bang sticks on the pond to try and break a chink in the ice. But it was frozen deep, deep down as far as they could see, and it only chipped a little and bright, hard slivers flew up like glass.

By the time Father came out of the cottage and they set off for home again, Fanny's cheeks felt as if they were on fire in the coldness of the air, but it had been a very long time since her breakfast, and along the lane beyond the fork, her legs felt suddenly very tired, as if they would not carry her, and her head was buzzing. So then they stood in the shelter of the high hedge, and Father took a little paper package of muscatel raisins from deep in his pocket, and they shared them together, and rested until Fanny was quite ready to go on. And nothing, she thought, nothing, nothing, had ever tasted so sweet and good in her life.

But the best thing of all to happen that whole Christmas was still to come, and until they had reached home, and Fanny had taken off her outdoor clothes and washed her hands, and sat down to the luncheon table, not a word was said about it, it was the most complete and perfect surprise. Though as soon as she saw him, she knew that brother Will had a secret, his face was brilliant with it, he smiled and smiled, and kept looking at Fanny, and then at Mother, and smiling again, and shuffling and tapping his feet and nodding his head, until he was frowned at to be still.

But her mother looked pleased, too, Fanny thought, and full of the same private knowledge.

First, though, she herself had to tell, about the walk and about how she had gone to say goodbye to Seth Locke, and about holding the Tumney baby. And as she talked, and listened as Father talked, and ate her meat and drank her milk, tiredness began to seep into her limbs again; she felt as if she were being covered over with a thick, soft, heavy counterpane, and all their voices sounded farther and farther away.

Then, looking sharply at her, her mother said, 'Time to tell' to Will, and Will sat bolt upright, and Father looked from one to the other of them, for explanation. And Will said very slowly, 'While you were gone to the village, a message was brought.'

Fanny watched his face intently.

'A message from m'lord at the Hall. And the message was an invitation to Mr Hart, the Rector, and to the Rector's wife, and the Rector's son.'

He looked teasingly across the table at Fanny, and paused, and took a long, slow drink from his water-glass, and set it down carefully again.

'And *even* to Miss Hart, the Rector's daughter . . . oh, imagine that!'

But Fanny felt too tired to be impatient with him. She just sat in half a dream, and saw the white world beyond the windows, and the blackbird as it went hop-hop-hop across the snow, and waited.

'We are invited to a party from six o'clock this very evening. At the Hall. An illuminated skating party on the lake, which has frozen hard as hard, with music. And refreshments. And all manner of delights!'

Then Will stood up and waved his hands in the air, and said, 'And isn't *that* the grandest thing, little Fanny!' and then he came round to her chair, and pulled her off it, and danced her around and around, and Fanny saw how his eyes shone and caught his own excitement in spite of her tiredness, and let him jig her up and down the room, while Mother and Father looked on and smiled, at them, and at one another.

But then, Mother stood up and came over and took Fanny's hand.

'Bed,' she said. 'Sleep, if you are to be allowed to a skating party, *after dark!*'

And Fanny went with her very willingly, and wondered only if her legs would carry her to the top of the stairs. When she undressed, and slipped into her bed, she felt down to find that the hot stone water bottle had been put there.

'Wake me up,' she said, watching her mother draw the curtains across to shut out the bright daylight. 'Don't go there without me.'

'No,' her mother said, and bent to stroke Fanny's hair, 'oh, no!'

And Fanny slept, and did not even hear her close the door behind her.

'After this morning,' Fanny said, as she was doing up her coat in the hall, and her fingers were all thumbs and the right holes matched the wrong buttons, 'after this morning, my legs felt so tired I thought they might never go properly again. But now . . .' and she did a few steps on the flagged floor, 'now, I could run and run and dance and dance, and walk for a hundred miles.'

'Only you won't have to walk for a hundred miles, or even for one,' Will said. 'And that is another thing you didn't know, but *I* knew.'

'What do you mean? Oh, tell, Will, *tell* . . .'

69

But what Will did was not tell anything, but instead, he listened, and then said 'There!' And Fanny heard it too, a noise outside in the drive, the sound of wheels, and of stamping.

'There!' said Will. 'We are sent for!' and he flung open the door. And there, outside in the snow, stood the trap from the Hall, pulled by one of the grey ponies, and with Dorkin, the younger groom, at the reins.

Then Father and Mother, and Will and Fanny stepped out into the snow, and behind them in the hallway, Nancy and Kate came to admire, and to wave them off, and after Fanny had stepped up into the trap and had sat down, Dorkin tucked a rug around her. She looked up and saw that the night sky was pricked all over with bright, bright stars, and the moon was round as a pumpkin and pale as silk, and it shone full onto the snow so that they could see as well as in the brightness of day.

And as they set off, she pinched herself, in wonder, that this was real, and she herself a true and living part of it.

The Hall stood quite close to the Rectory, at the end of a long avenue of elm trees. But tonight, they took the road that wound around away from the house, through a copse, and then out into the clearing to where there was a dip. And in the dip, surrounded by sloping grassy banks, lay the Lake.

As they drew near to it, looking ahead, Fanny saw lights flickering, yellow and white and green and red and blue, like a rainbow in the darkness, and then the Lake lay before them, frozen, glittering, unearthly under the rising moon. And set all around it on poles in the grass were Chinese lanterns, and in other places, fires, logs set within iron hurdles, and blazing bright, and right on the edge of the ice were two great braziers, glowing like the smithy's forge, and sending showers of white sparks flying up into the night sky.

Already people were skating, in pairs and singly, and then m'lord and lady were welcoming them, and Mother and Father were thanking and talking and, catching her eye, Will gave Fanny a great wink of delight.

There were benches laid out with spare skates and boots, for any who had not their own, and, seeing the brightness and sharpness of the blades, Fanny hesitated, suddenly afraid of them, and of the great, shining expanse of the frozen lake. But Father and Will said they would take her between them and hold her up, and so they did. She went very carefully and safely around the edge, but in a little while, grew bolder, and set her feet down more firmly, one-two, one-two, and felt the cold air on her face, and heard the blades hiss-hiss.

Only it was quite difficult, after all, and cold, too; she could not skate for long, so they brought her back to sit close to one of the braziers, and watch Mother and Father skate off beautifully over the ice, with hands linked, across.

Then came the music from the other side of the lake. The band which had been setting itself up began suddenly to play, and more and more people were arriving and taking to the ice, and they skated the Quadrille and the Lancers, and then there was a pause before the band played a gallop that got faster and faster, so that the blades of the skaters skimmed and flew and hardly seemed to touch the ice, and Fanny saw her mother go past with her eyes shining, and her muffler streaming behind her. Some people were skating with torches, holding them up so that they flared and flickered, and made trails like fiery comets in the darkness.

And the coloured lanterns swung and shone, and made bright watery pools of light on the ice, and the air was sweet with the smell of wood smoke and roasting chestnuts and it was cold, cold, and the sound of the music and the laughter, the calling voices and the whip-whip of the skate blades all began to swirl and dance before Fanny's eyes. It was as if the whole world was spinning, and caught up in the movement of the skating and the beauty of the moonlight and the torchlight and the lantern light on the ice of the lake, and the snow-covered banks all around.

She thought she had never been so happy in all her life, never felt so joyful and light of heart, that there had never been such magic in the world, such wonder, such a Christmas.

And suddenly, she stood up and, in the snow, began to dance to the music, to hold out her arms to the lanterns and the glowing fires and the skaters, and her head was light and the earth spun like a top, and she looked all around her and then, at last, up at all the stars in the sky. And very quietly, in a whisper, she said, 'Oh, glory, glory!' so that only she herself could hear.

'Oh glory, glory, glory!'

And much later, riding home again in the trap, Fanny felt more wide awake than she ever had done in her life, and as though she were seeing everything for the first time.

The fields were bone-white, and completely empty and still, and the grey coat and mane of the pony gleamed and the harness glinted now and then, and the trees arched over them as they drove through the copse. And, looking up between their silver branches, Fanny saw the evening star, the brightest and strongest of all, and as they turned out into the lane, it stayed just ahead of them, to lead their way home.

AFTERWORD

LAST NIGHT, the snow fell. And then I began to remember. And today is Christmas Eve, and still it snows, and still I go on remembering, and the memories will keep me company.

I sit here, beside the window, and watch the snow, and the blackbird who comes and sits under the flowering bush, and after a while hops out further, to find the food that I have thrown. The yellow flowers of the bush are dusted with snow, and the bare branches of the tall tree are outlined delicately in white. And I sit here, beside the window, and my lamp throws its light in a pool onto the ground below, but there is no snow so close to the building, the overhang of the roof above deflects it.

And all last night, and all today, I have sat here quietly and remembered. Remembered joy and sorrow, nights and days, summer and winter, in that perfect place.

I remember my room at the very top of the tall old

house, and the view out over the churchyard, and the gravestone of my two dead brothers. Remember the stone church and the fields beyond, remember the wood and the lanes and Ladyman Barrow.

And Nancy in the Rectory kitchen, and Sam Hay who whistled through the gap in his teeth. And m'lord at the Hall, and my lady. Old Betsy Barlow with one leg, Pether the church-warden. And Mr Vale, the verger, Father's right hand. And his curate with the bobbing Adam's-apple and the new, new wife.

Father, and Mother, and brother Will.

Last night, the snow fell, and I began to remember. Today it is Christmas Eve. And I remember that Christmas best of all, when I was nine years old, and the snow lay like a goose-down quilt over the earth, and I walked across the churchyard, through the deep, soft drifts, to listen to Father say Evensong, by the light of the candles.

I remember the carol singers coming with their lanterns across the snow, and their voices, and the sound of the flute and the fiddle. Remember sitting on the stairs with brother Will, and our mother handing around the plate of mince pies in the hall below, and not looking up at us or noticing.

And in the kitchen the sweet rich smells and the dark, dark fruit in the china bowl, and a cat on a cushion and a lemon rolling onto the stone-flagged floor.

Remember sleeping and waking in the thin blue light of Christmas morning. And the great stoves blazing in the icy church, and the brown savoury skin of the roasted fowl, and the death of Seth Locke and the birth of Thomas Tumney's baby; and on St Stephen's Day, the stiff dead body of the tiny frozen shrew, the feel of Seth Locke's hand to my warm touch, and the new, new baby in the crook of my arm.

And the skating with torches, and the great, great beauty of that snow-covered world.

I remember. For that was the last country Christmas. The next spring, Father was made a canon of the Cathedral and we went away, away from the Rectory and the little stone church, and the grave of our two dead brothers; away from the fields and the wood, the lanes and the stream and the ditches, and the great wide barrow. Away from the country to the city, where we were happy enough in another tall house, joined to a row of others and set in the Close, but where our life ever after was so very, very different.

And after that, it seemed, I left behind my childhood, that magic time, set within a circle and lit from within, so that the memory of it, coming to me down all the years, is golden as the light of a lantern falling across the snow.